THE STORIES
MOTHER NATURE
TOLD HER CHILDREN

JANE ANDREWS

1st WORLD
LIBRARY
Literary Society

The Stories Mother Nature Told Her Children

Jane Andrews

© 1st World Library – Literary Society, 2004
PO Box 2211
Fairfield, IA 52556
www.1stworldlibrary.org
First Edition

LCCN: 2004195323

Softcover ISBN: 1-4218-0154-X
Hardcover ISBN: 1-4218-0054-3
eBook ISBN: 1-4218-0254-6

Purchase *"The Stories Mother Nature Told Her Children"*
as a traditional bound book at:
www.1stWorldLibrary.org/purchase.asp?ISBN=1-4218-0154-X

1st World Library Literary Society is a nonprofit
organization dedicated to promoting literacy by:

- Creating a free internet library accessible from any
  computer worldwide.
- Hosting writing competitions and offering book
  publishing scholarships.

The Stories Mother Nature Told Her Children
contributed by Tim, Ed & Rodney
in support of
1st World Library Literary Society

CONTENTS

THE STORY OF THE AMBER BEADS 7

THE NEW LIFE.. 12

THE TALK OF THE TREES THAT STAND IN
THE VILLAGE STREET 17

HOW THE INDIAN CORN GROWS 23

WATER-LILIES 26

THE CARRYING TRADE 29

THE SEA-LIFE... 35

WHAT THE FROST GIANTS DID TO NANNIE'S RUN 50

HOW QUERCUS ALBA WENT TO EXPLORE THE
UNDERWORLD, AND WHAT CAME OF IT...................... 57

A PEEP INTO ONE OF GOD'S STOREHOUSES 70

THE HIDDEN LIGHT 78

SIXTY-TWO LITTLE TADPOLES 81

GOLDEN-ROD AND ASTERS 86

THE STORY OF THE AMBER BEADS

Do you know Mother Nature? She it is to whom God has given the care of the earth, and all that grows in or upon it, just as he has given to your mother the care of her family of boys and girls.

You may think that Mother Nature, like the famous "old woman who lived in the shoe," has so many children that she doesn't know what to do. But you will know better when you become acquainted with her, and learn how strong she is, and how active; how she can really be in fifty places at once, taking care of a sick tree, or a baby flower just born; and, at the same time, building underground palaces, guiding the steps of little travellers setting out on long journeys, and sweeping, dusting, and arranging her great house, - the earth. And all the while, in the midst of her patient and never-ending work, she will tell us the most charming and marvellous stories of ages ago when she was young, or of the treasures that lie hidden in the most distant and secret closets of her palace; just such stories as you all like so well to hear your mother tell when you gather round her in the twilight.

A few of these stories which she has told to me, I am about to tell you, beginning with this one.

I know a little Scotch girl: she lives among the

Highlands. Her home is hardly more than a hut; her food, broth and bread. Her father keeps sheep on the hillsides; and, instead of wearing a coat, wraps himself in his plaid, for protection from the cold winds that drive before them great clouds of mist and snow among the mountains.

As for Jeanie herself (you must be careful to spell her name with an ea, for that is Scotch fashion), her yellow hair is bound about with a little snood; her face is browned by exposure to the weather; and her hands are hardened by work, for she helps her mother to cook and sew, to spin and weave.

One treasure little Jeanie has which many a lady would be proud to wear. It is a necklace of amber beads, - "lamour beads," old Elsie calls them; that is the name they went by when she was young.

You have, perhaps, seen amber, and know its rich, sunshiny color, and its fragrance when rubbed; and do you also know that rubbing will make amber attract things somewhat as a magnet does? Jeanie's beads had all these properties, but some others besides, wonderful and lovely; and it is of those particularly that I wish to tell you. Each bead has inside of it some tiny thing, incased as if it had grown in the amber; and Jeanie is never tired of looking at, and wondering about, them. Here is one with a delicate bit of ferny moss shut up, as it were, in a globe of yellow light. In another is the tiniest fly, - his little wings outspread, and raised for flight. Again, she can show us a bee lodged in one bead that looks like solid honey, and a little bright-winged beetle in another. This one holds two slender pine-needles lying across each other, and here we see a single scale of a pine-cone; while yet another shows an

Jane Andrews

atom of an acorn-cup, fit for a fairy's use. I wish you could see the beads, for I cannot tell you the half of their beauty. Now, where do you suppose they came from, and how did little Scotch Jeanie come into possession of such a treasure?

All she knows about it is, that her grandfather, - old Kenneth, who cowers now all day in the chimney-corner, - once, years ago when he was a young lad, went down upon the seashore after a great storm, hoping to help save something from the wreck of the "Goshawk," that had gone ashore during the night; and there among the slippery seaweeds his foot had accidentally uncovered a clear, shining lump of amber, in which all these little creatures were embedded. Now, Kenneth loved a pretty Highland lass; and, when she promised to be his bride, he brought her a necklace of amber beads. He had carved them himself out of his lump of amber, working carefully to save in each bead the prettiest insect or moss, and thinking, while he toiled hour after hour, of the delight with which he should see his bride wear them. That bride was Jeanie's grandmother; and when she died last year, she said, "Let little Jeanie have my lamour beads, and keep them as long as she lives."

But what puzzled Jeanie was, how the amber came to be on the seashore; and, most of all, how the bees and mosses came inside of it. Should you like to know? If you would, that is one of Mother Nature's stories, and she will gladly tell it. Hear what she answers to our questions: -

"I remember a time, long, long before you were born, - long, even, before any men were living upon the earth; then these Scotch Highlands, as you call them, where little Jeanie lives, were covered with forests. There were oaks, poplars, beeches, and pines; and among them one kind of pine, tall and stately, from which a shining yellow gum flowed, just as you have seen little drops of sticky gum exude from our own pine-trees. This beautiful yellow gum was fragrant; and, as the thousands of little insects fluttered about it in the warm sunshine, they were attracted by its pleasant odor, - perhaps, too, by its taste, - and once alighted upon it, they stuck fast, and could not get away; while the great yellow drops oozing out surrounded, and at last covered, them entirely. So, too, wind-blown bits of moss, leaves, acorns, cones, and little sticks were soon securely imbedded in the fast-flowing gum; and, as time went by, it hardened and hardened more and more. And this is amber."

"That is well told, Mother Nature; but it does not explain how Kenneth's lump of amber came to be on the seashore."

"Wait, then, for the second part of the story.

"Did you ever hear that, in those very old times, the land sometimes sank down into the sea, even so deep that the water covered the very mountain-tops; and then, after ages, it was slowly lifted up again, to sink indeed, perhaps, yet again and again?

"You can hardly believe it, yet I myself was there to see; and I remember well when the great forests of the North of Scotland - the oaks, the poplars, and the amber-pines - were lowered into the deep sea. There, lying at the bottom of the ocean, the wood and the gum hardened like stone, and only the great storms can disturb them as they lie half buried in the sand. It was

Jane Andrews

one of those great storms that brought Kenneth's lump of amber to land."

If we could only walk on the bottom of the sea, what treasures we might find!

THE NEW LIFE

It is May, - almost the end of May, indeed, and the Mayflowers have finished their blooming for this year. It is growing too warm for those delicate violets and hepaticas who dare to brave even March winds, and can bear snow better than summer heats.

Down at the edge of the pond the tall water-grasses and rushes are tossing their heads a little in the wind, and swinging a little, lightly and lazily, with the motion of the water; but the water is almost clear and still this morning, scarcely rippled, and in its beautiful, broad mirror reflecting the chestnut-trees on the bank, and the little points of land that run out from the shore, and give foothold to the old pines standing guard day and night, summer and winter, to watch up the pond and down.

Do you think now that you know how the pond looks in the sunshine of this May morning?

If we come close to the edge where the rushes are growing, and look down through the clear water, we shall see some uncouth and clumsy black bugs crawling upon the bottom of the pond. They have six legs, and are covered with a coat of armor laid plate over plate. It looks hard and horny; and the insect himself has a dull, heavy way with him, and might be

Jane Andrews

called very stupid were it not for his eagerness in catching and eating every little fly and mosquito that comes within his reach. His eyes grow fierce and almost bright; and he seizes with open mouth, and devours all day long, if he can find any thing suited to his taste.

I am afraid you will think he is not very interesting, and will not care to make his acquaintance. But, let me tell you, something very wonderful is about to happen to him; and if you stay and watch patiently, you will see what I saw once, and have never forgotten.

Here he is crawling in mud under the water this May morning: out over the pond shoot the flat water-boatmen, and the water-spiders dance and skip as if the pond were a floor of glass; while here and there skims a blue dragon-fly, with his fine, firm wings that look like the thinnest gauze, but are really wondrously strong for all their delicate appearance.

The dull, black bug sees all these bright, agile insects; and, for the first time in his life, he feels discontented with his own low place in the mud. A longing creeps through him that is quite different from the customary longing for mosquitoes and flies. "I will creep up the stem of this rush," he thinks; "and perhaps, when I reach the surface of the water, I can dart like the little flat boatmen, or, better than all, shoot through the air like the blue-winged dragon-fly." But, as he crawls toilsomely up the slippery stem, the feeling that he has no wings like the dragon-fly makes him discouraged and almost despairing. At last, however, with much labor he has reached the surface, has crept out of the water, and, clinging to the green stem, feels the spring air and sunshine all about him. Now let him take passage with the boatmen, or ask some of the little spiders to dance. Why doesn't he begin to enjoy himself?

Alas! see his sad disappointment. After all this toil, after passing some splendid chances of good breakfasts on the way up, and spending all his strength on this one exploit, he finds the fresh air suffocating him, and a most strange and terrible feeling coming over him, as his coat-of-mail, which until now was always kept wet, shrinks, and seems even cracking off while the warm air dries it.

"Oh," thinks the poor bug, "I must die! It was folly in me to crawl up here. The mud and the water were good enough for my brothers, and good enough for me too, had I only known it; and now I am too weak, and feel too strangely, to attempt going down again the way I came up."

See how uneasy he grows, feeling about in doubt and dismay, for a darkness is coming over his eyes. It is the black helmet, a part of his coat-of-mail; it has broken off at the top, and is falling down over his face. A minute more, and it drops below his chin; and what is his astonishment to find, that, as his old face breaks away, a new one comes in its place, larger, much more beautiful, and having two of the most admirable eyes! - two, I say, because they look like two, but each of them is made up of hundreds of little eyes. They stand out globe-like on each side of his head, and look about over a world unknown and wonderful to the dull, black bug who lived in the mud. The sky seems bluer, the sunshine brighter, and the nodding grass and flowers more gay and graceful. Now he lifts this new head to see more of the great world; and behold! as he moves,

Jane Andrews

he is drawing himself out of the old suit of armor, and from two neat little cases at its sides come two pairs of wings, folded up like fans, and put away here to be ready for use when the right time should come: still half folded they are, and must be carefully spread open and smoothed for use. And while he trembles with surprise, see how with every movement he is escaping from the old armor, and drawing from their sheaths fine legs, longer and far more beautifully made and colored than the old; and a slender body that was packed away like a spy-glass, and is now drawn slowly out, one part after another; until at last the dark coat-of-mail dangles empty from the rushes, and above it sits a dragon-fly with great, wondering eyes, long, slender body, and two pairs of delicate, gauzy wings, - fine and firm as the very ones he had been watching but an hour ago.

The poor black bug who thought he was dying was only passing out of his old life to be born into a higher one; and see how much brighter and more beautiful it is!

And now shall I tell you how, months ago, the mother dragon-fly dropped into the water her tiny eggs, which lay there in the mud, and by and by hatched out the dark, crawling bugs, so unlike the mother that she does not know them for her children, and, flying over the pond, looks down through the water where they crawl among the rushes, and has not a single word to say to them; until, in due time, they find their way up to the air, and pass into the new winged life.

If you will go to some pond when spring is ending or summer beginning, and find among the water-grasses such an insect as I have told you of, you may see all this for yourselves; and you will say with me, dear children, that nothing you have ever known is more wonderful.

Jane Andrews

THE TALK OF THE TREES THAT STAND
IN THE VILLAGE STREET

How still it is! Nobody in the village street, the children all at school, and the very dogs sleeping lazily in the sunshine. Only a south wind blows lightly through the trees, lifting the great fans of the horse-chestnut, tossing the slight branches of the elm against the sky like single feathers of a great plume, and swinging out fragrance from the heavy-hanging linden-blossoms.

Through the silence there is a little murmur, like a low song. It is the song of the trees: each has its own voice, which may be known from all others by the ear that has learned how to listen.

The topmost branches of the elm are talking of the sky, - of those highest white clouds that float like tresses of silver hair in the far blue, of the sunrise gold and the rose-color of sunset that always rest upon them most lovingly. But down deep in the heart of the great branches you may hear something quite different, and not less sweet.

"Peep under my leaves," sings the elm-tree, "out at the ends of my broadest branches. What hangs there so soft and gray? Who comes with a flash of wings and gleam of golden breast among the dark leaves, and sits above the gray hanging nest to sing his full, sweet tune? Who worked there together so happily all the May-time, with gray honeysuckle fibres, twining the little nest, until there it hung securely over the road, bound and tied and woven firmly to the slender twigs? so slender that the squirrels even cannot creep down for the eggs; much less can Jack or Neddy, who are so fond of birds'-nesting, ever hope to reach the home of our golden robin.

"There my leaves shelter him like a roof from rain and from sunshine. I rock the cradle when the father and mother are away and the little ones cry, and in my softest tone I sing to them; yet they are never quite satisfied with me, but beat their wings, and stretch out their heads, and cannot be happy until they hear their father.

"The squirrel, who lives in the hole where the two great branches part, hears what I say, and curls up his tail, while he turns his bright eyes towards the swinging nest which he can never reach."

The fanning wind wafts across the road the voice of the old horse-chestnut, who also has a word to say about the birds'-nests.

"When my blossoms were fresh, white pyramids, came a swift flutter of wings about them one day, and a dazzlingly beautiful little bird thrust his long, delicate bill among the flowers; and while he held himself there in the air without touching his tiny feet to twig or stem, but only by the swift fanning of long, green-tinted wings, I offered him my best flowers for his breakfast, and bowed my great leaves as a welcome to him. The dear little thing had been here before, while yet the sticky brown buds which wrap up my leaves had not burst open to the warm sunshine. He and his mate, whose feather dress was not so fine as his, gathered the gum from the outside of the buds, and pulled the warm wool from the inside; and I could watch them as they flew away to the maple yonder, for then the trees that stand between us had no leaves to hide the maple, as they do now.

"Back and forth flew the birds from the topmost maple-branch to my opening buds; and day by day I saw a little nest growing, very small and round, lined warmly with wool from my buds, and thatched all over the outside with bits of lichen, gray and green, to match what grew on the maple-branches about it; and this thatch was glued on with the gum from my brown buds. When it was finished, it was delicate enough for the cradle of a little princess, and the outside was so carefully matched to the tree by lichens, that the sharpest eyes from below could not detect it. What a safe, snug home for the humming-birds!

"By the time the two tiny eggs were laid, I could no longer see the nest, for the thick foliage of other trees had built up a green wall between me and it. But for many days the mother-bird staid away, and the father came alone to drink honey from my blossom-cups: so I knew that the eggs were hatching under her warm folded wings, for I have seen such things before among my own branches in the robins' nests and the bluebirds'.

"Now my flowers are all gone, and in their place the nuts are growing in their prickly balls. I have nothing to tempt the humming-bird, and he never visits me: only the yellow birds hop gayly from branch to branch, and the robins come sometimes." And the horse-chestnut sighed, for he missed the humming-bird; and he flapped his great leaves in the very face of the linden-blossoms, and forgot to say "Excuse me." But the linden is now, and for many days, full of sweetness, and will not answer ungraciously even so careless a touch.

Yes, the linden is full of sweetness, and sends out the fragrance from his blossoms in through the chamber windows, and down upon the people who pass in the street below. And he tells all the time his story of how his pink-covered leaf-buds opened in the spring mornings, and unfolded the fresh green leaves, which were so tender and full of green juices that it was no wonder the mother-moth had thought the branches a good place whereon to lay her eggs; for as soon as they should be all laid, she would die, and there would be no one to provide food for her babies when they should creep out.

"So the nice mother-moth made a toilsome journey up my great trunk," sung the linden, "and left her eggs where she knew the freshest green leaves would be coming out by the time the young ones should leave the eggs.

"And they came out indeed, somewhat to my sorrow; for instead of being, like their mother, sober, well-behaved little moths, they were green canker-worms, and such hungry little things, that I really began to fear I should have not a whole leaf left upon me; when one day they spun for themselves fine silken ropes, and swung themselves down from leaf to leaf, and from branch to branch, and in a day or two were all gone.

"A little flaxen-haired girl sat on the broad doorstep at my feet, and caught the canker-worms in her white apron. She liked to see them hump up their backs, and measure off the inches of her white checked apron with their little green bodies. And I, although I liked them well enough at first, was not sorry to lose them when they went. I heard the child's mother telling her that they had come down to make for themselves beds in the earth, where they would sleep until the early spring, and wake to find themselves grown into moths just like their mothers, who climbed up the tree to lay eggs. We shall see when next spring comes if that is so. Now, since they went, I have done my best to refresh my leaves, and keep young and happy; and here are my sweet blossoms to prove that I have yet within me vigorous life."

The elm-tree heard what the linden sung, and said, "Very true, very true. I, too, have suffered from the canker-worms; but I have yet leaves enough left for a beautiful shade, and the poor crawling things must surely eat something." And the elm bowed gracefully to the linden, out of sympathy for him.

But the linden has heard the voices of the young robins who live in the nest among his highest boughs; and he must yet tell to the horse-chestnut how sad it was the other day in the thunder-storm, when the wind upset the nest, and one little bird was thrown out and killed; while the father and mother flew about in the greatest distress, until Charley came, climbed the tree, and fitted the nest safely back into its place.

How much the trees have to say! And there is the pine, who was born and brought up in the woods, - he is always whispering secrets of the great forest, and of the river beside which he grew. The other trees can't always understand him: he is the poet among them, and a poet is always suspected of knowing a little more than any one else.

Sometime I may try to tell you something of what he says; but here ends the talk of the trees that stood in the village street.

HOW THE INDIAN CORN GROWS

The children came in from the field with their hands full of the soft, pale-green corn-silk. Annie had rolled hers into a bird's-nest; while Willie had dressed his little sister's hair with the long, damp tresses, until she seemed more like a mermaid, with pale blue eyes shining out between the locks of her sea-green hair, than like our own Alice.

They brought their treasures to the mother, who sat on the door-step of the farm-house, under the tall, old elm-tree that had been growing there ever since her mother was a child. She praised the beauty of the bird's-nest, and kissed the little mermaiden to find if her lips tasted of salt water; but then she said, "Don't break any more of the silk, dear children, else we shall have no ears of corn in the field, - none to roast before our picnic fires, and none to dry and pop at Christmas-time next winter."

Now, the children wondered at what their mother said, and begged that she would tell them how the silk could make the round, full kernels of corn. And this is the story that the mother told, while they all sat on the door-step under the old elm.

"When your father broke up the ground with his plough, and scattered in the seed-corn, the crows were watching from the old apple-tree, and they came down to pick up the corn; and, indeed, they did carry away a good deal. But the days went by, the spring showers moistened the earth, and the sun shone; and so the seed-corn swelled, and, bursting open, thrust out two little hands, one reaching down to hold itself firmly in the earth, and one reaching up to the light and air. The first was never very beautiful, but certainly quite useful; for, besides holding the corn firmly in its place, it drew up water and food for the whole plant: but the second spread out two long, slender green leaves, that waved with every breath of air, and seemed to rejoice in every ray of sunshine. Day by day it grew taller and taller, and by and by put out new streamers broader and stronger, until it stood higher than Willie's head. Then, at the top, came a new kind of bud, quite different from those that folded the green streamers; and when that opened, it showed a nodding flower, which swayed and bowed at the top of the stalk like the crown of the whole plant. And yet this was not the best that the corn-plant could do; for lower down, and partly hidden by the leaves, it had hung out a silken tassel of pale sea-green color, like the hair of a little mermaid. Now, every silken thread was in truth a tiny tube, so fine that our eyes cannot see the bore of it. The nodding flower that grew so gayly up above there was day by day ripening a golden dust called pollen; and every grain of this pollen - and they were very small grains indeed - knew perfectly well that the silken threads were tubes, and they felt an irresistible desire to enter the shining passages, and explore them to the very end: so one day, when the wind was tossing the whole blossoms this way and that, the pollen-grains danced out, and, sailing down on the soft breeze, each one crept in at the open door of a sea-green tube. Down they slid over the shining floors; and what was their delight to find, when they reached the end, that they had all along been expected, and for each one was a little room prepared, and sweet food for their nourishment! And from this time they had no desire to go away, but remained each in his own place, and grew every day stronger and larger and rounder, even as baby in the cradle there, who has nothing to do but grow.

"Side by side were their cradles, one beyond another in beautiful straight rows; and as the pollen-grains grew daily larger, the cradles also grew for their accommodation, until at last they felt themselves really full of sweet, delicious life; and those who lived at the tops of the rows peeped out from the opening of the dry leaves which wrapped them all together, and saw a little boy with his father coming through the cornfield, while yet every thing was beaded with dew, and the sun was scarcely an hour high. The boy carried a basket; and the father broke from the corn-stalks the full, firm ears of sweet corn, and heaped the basket full."

"O mother," cried Willie, "that was father and I! Don't you remember how we used to go out last summer every morning before breakfast to bring in the corn? And we must have taken that very ear; for I remember how the full kernels lay in straight rows, side by side, just as you have told."

Now Alice is breaking her threads of silk, and trying to see the tiny opening of the tube; and Annie thinks she will look for the pollen-grains the very next time she goes to the cornfield.

WATER-LILIES

The stream that crept down from the hills, three miles away, has worn a smooth bed for itself in the gravel; has watered the farmer's fields, and turned the wheel of the old grist-mill, where the miller tends the stones that grind the farmer's corn. But down below here the stream has something else to do. It has been working hard, up and away from dam to dam again; and as always in life there should be something besides business, - something beautiful and peaceful, - so the stream has swept round this corner, behind the wooded point of land which hides the mill, and spread itself out in the hollow of Brown's meadow, where farmer Brown says his grandfather used to tell him some Indian wigwams stood when he was a boy. The land has sunk since then, and there is something more beautiful than Indian wigwams there now.

Where the old squaws used to sit weaving baskets, and the papooses rolled and played, is now thick, black mud, in which are great tangled roots, some of them bigger than my arm.

All winter they lie there under the ice, while the children skate over them. In the spring, when every thing stirs with new life, they, too, must wake up: so, slowly and steadily, they begin to put up long stems to reach the surface of the water. Chambered stems they

Jane Andrews

are, each having four passages leading up to the air, and down to the root and black mud. The walls of these chambers are brown and slimy, and each stem bears at its top a slimy bud, - slimy on the outside, brownish-green as it pushes up through the water; for this outer coat is stout and waterproof, and can well afford to be unpretending, since it carries something very precious wrapped up inside.

Not days, but weeks, - even months, it is working upon this hidden treasure before we shall see it. And the July mornings have come while we wait.

Can you wake at three o'clock, children, and, while the birds are singing their very best songs, go down the road under the elms, across the little bridge, and through the hemlock grove at the right? It is a mile to walk, and you will not be there too early. The broad, smooth pond, that the brook has made for its holiday pleasure, is at our feet. At its bottom are the tangled roots; on the surface, among the flat, green leaves, float those buds that have been so long creeping towards the light.

One long, bright beam from the sun just rising smiles across the meadow, and touches the folded buds. They must, indeed, smile back in reply; so the thick sheath unfolds, and behold! the whitest, fairest lily-cup floats on the water, and its golden centre smiles back to the sun with many rays.

We watched only one, but perhaps none is willing to be latest in greeting the sun, and the pond is already half-covered with a snowy fleet of boats fit for the fairies, - boats under full sail for fairy-land, laden with beauty and fragrance.

And this is what the dark mud can send forth. This is one of Mother Nature's hidden treasures. Perhaps she hides something as white and beautiful in all that seems dark and ugly, if only we will wait and watch for it, and be willing to come at the very dawn of day to look for it.

The lilies will stay with us, now that at last they are here, all through the rest of the summer, and even into the warm, sunny days of earliest October; but it will be only a few who stay so late as that And where have the others gone, meanwhile? You see there are no dead lilies floating, folded and decaying, among the pads.

The stem that found its way so surely to the upper world knows not less surely the way back again; and when its white blossom has opened for the last time, and then wrapped its green cloak about it again, not to be unfolded, the chambered stem coils backward, and carries it safely to the bottom, where its seed may ripen in the soft, dark mud, and prepare for another summer.

Jane Andrews

THE CARRYING TRADE

Who wants to engage in the carrying trade? Come, Lottie and Lula and Nina and Mary, all bring your maps, and we will play merchants, and see what is meant by the carrying trade.

Lottie shall have the bark "Rosette," and sail from Boston to Calcutta; Lula, the steamer "North Star," from New York for Liverpool; Mary shall take the "Sea-Gull," from Philadelphia to San Francisco; and Nina is owner of the "Racer," that makes voyages up the Mediterranean. Are we all ready for our little game?

Lottie begins, and she must find out what Boston has to send to Calcutta. Don't send indigo or saltpetre or gunny-bags or ginger; for, even should you have these articles to spare, Calcutta has an abundance at home, and you must discover something that she needs, but does not possess. "Ice," says Lottie. "Yes, that is just the thing, because Calcutta has a hot climate, and does not make her own ice: so load the 'Rosette' with great blocks well packed, and start at once, for your voyage is long."

And now we will go with Lula to the North River pier, where her great steamer lies, and see what she intends to carry to Liverpool. Bales of cotton, barrels of flour, of beef, and of petroleum. All very good, so good-by to her. In a few weeks we will see what she brings back.

Come, Mary, what has Philadelphia for San Francisco? Oh, what a load the "Sea-Gull" must take of machinery, steam-engines, tobacco, and oil; and such a quantity of other things, that the "Sea-Gull" will need to make many voyages before she can take them all. We load her at this busy wharf, where the coal-vessels are passing in and out for New York and Boston, and the steamers are loading for Europe, and the little coasters crowding in one after another; and away we go for the voyage round the "Horn," where the "Sea-Gull" will meet her namesakes, and perhaps some stormy winds besides.

Meantime Nina's "Racer" has been stored full of cotton cloths and hardware, and has raced out of Boston Harbor so swiftly that fair winds will take her to Gibraltar in three weeks.

And so you have all engaged in the carrying trade; but as yet you have carried only one way. To complete the game, we must wait for Lottie to bring the "Rosette" safely home with salt-petre and indigo and hides and ginger and seersuckers and gunny-cloth. And the "North Star" must steam her quick way across the Atlantic, and return with salt and hardware, anchors, steel, woolens, and linens. Mary must beat her way round Cape Horn, and home again with wool and gold and silver. And the swift "Racer" must quickly bring the figs and prunes and raisins, and the oranges and lemons, that will spoil if they are too long on the way.

So children may play at the carrying trade, and so their fathers and uncles may work at it in earnest: and so also hundreds of little workers are busy all the world over in another carrying trade, which keeps you and me alive from day to day; and yet we scarcely think; at all how it is going on, or stop to thank the hands that feed us.

England and Italy are kingdoms, and the United States a republic, and they all engage in this business, and are constantly sending goods one to another; but there are other kingdoms, not put down on any map, that are just as busy as they, and in the same sort of work too.

The earth is one kingdom, the water another, and there is the great republic of the gases surrounding us on every side; only we can't see it, because its inhabitants have the fairy gift of being invisible to us. Each of these kingdoms has products to export, and is all ready to trade with the others, if only some one will supply the means; just as the Frenchmen might stand on their shores, and hold out to us wines and prunes and silks and muslins, and we might stand on our shores, and hold out gold and silver to them, and yet could make no exchange, because there were no ships to carry the goods across. "Ah," you may say, "that is not at all the case here; for the earth, the air, and the water are all close to each other, and close to us, and there is no need of ships; we can exchange hand to hand."

But here comes a difficulty. Read carefully, and I think you will understand it. Here is Ruth, a little growing girl, who wants phosphate of lime to build bones with; for as she grows, of course her bones must grow too. Very well, I answer, there is plenty of phosphate of lime in the earth; she can have all she wants. Yes, but does Ruth want to eat earth? - do you? - does anybody? Certainly not: so, although the food she needs is close beside her, even under her feet, she cannot get it any more than we can get the French goods, excepting by means of the carrying trade. Where now are the little ships that shall bring to Ruth the phosphate of lime she needs, and cannot reach, although it lies in her own father's field? Let me show you how her father can build the ships that will bring it to her. He must go out into that field, and plant wheat-seeds, and as they grow, every little ear and kernel gathers up phosphate of lime, and becomes a tiny ship freighted with what his little daughter needs. When that wheat is ground into flour, and made into bread, Ruth will eat what she couldn't have been willing to taste, unless the useful little ships of the wheat-field had brought it to her.

Now let us send to the republic of the gases for some supplies, for we cannot live without carbon and oxygen; and although we do breathe in oxygen with every breathe we draw, we also need to receive it in other ways: so the sugar-cane and the maple-trees engage in the carrying trade for us, taking in carbon and oxygen by their leaves, and sending it through their bodies, and when it reaches us it is sugar, - and a very pleasant food to most of you, I dare say.

But we cannot take all we need of these gases in the form of sugar, and there are many other ships that will bring it to us. The corn will gather it up, and offer it in the form of meal, or of cornstarch puddings; or the grass will bring it to the cow, since you and I refuse to take it from the grass ships. But the cow offers it to us again in the form of milk, and we do not think of refusing; or the butcher offers it to us in the form of beef, and we do not say "no."

Alice wants some india-rubber shoes. Do you think the

kingdoms of air and water can send her a pair? The india-rubber tree in South America will take up water, and separate from it hydrogen, of which it is partly composed, and adding to this carbon from the air, will make a gum which we can work into shoes and balls, buttons, tubes, cups, cloth, and a hundred other useful articles.

Then, again, you and I, all of us, must go to the world of gases for nitrogen to help build our bodies, to make muscle and blood and skin and hair; and so the peas and beans load their boat-shaped seeds full, and bring it to us so fresh and excellent that we enjoy eating it.

This useful carrying trade has also another branch well worth looking at.

You remember hearing how many soldiers were sick in war-time at the South; but perhaps you do not know that their best medicine was brought to them by a South-American tree, that gathered up from the earth and air bitter juices to make what we call quinine. Then there is camphor, which I am sure you have all seen, sent by the East-Indian camphor-tree to cure you when you are sick; and gum-arabic and all the other gums; and castor-oil and most of the other medicines that you don't at all like, - all brought to us by the plants.

I might tell you a great deal more of this, but I will only stop to show a little what we give back in payment for all that is brought.

When England sends us hardware and woollen goods, she expects us to repay her with cotton and sugar, that are just as valuable to us as hardware and woolens to her; but see how differently we treat the kingdoms from which the plant-ships are all the time bringing us food and clothes and medicines, etc. All we return is just so much as we don't want to use. We take in good fresh air, and breathe out impure and bad. We throw back to the earth whatever will not nourish and strengthen us; and yet no complaint comes from the faithful plants. Do you wonder? I will let you into the secret of this. The truth is, that what is worthless to us is really just the food they need; and they don't at all know how little we value it ourselves. It is like the Chinese, of whom we might buy rice or silk or tea, and pay them in rats which we are glad to be rid of, while they consider them good food.

Now, I have given you only a peep into this carrying trade, but it is enough to show you how to use your own eyes to learn more about it. Look about you, and see if you can't tell as good a story as I have done, or a better one if you please.

THE SEA-LIFE

CHAPTER I.

THE STAR-FISH TAKES A SUMMER JOURNEY.

Once there was a little star-fish, and he had five fingers and five eyes, one at the end of each finger, - so that he might be said to have at least one power at his fingers' ends. And he had I can't tell you how many little feet; but being without legs, you see, he couldn't be expected to walk very fast The feet couldn't move one before the other as yours do. they could only cling like little suckers, by which he pulled himself slowly along from place to place. Nevertheless, he was very proud of this accomplishment; and sometimes this pride led him to an unjust contempt for his neighbors, as you will see by and by. He was very particular about his eating; and besides his mouth, which lay in the centre of his body, he had a little scarlet-colored sieve through which he strained the water he drank. For he couldn't think of taking in common seawater with every thing that might be floating in it, - that would do for crabs and lobsters and other common people; but anybody who wears such a lovely purple coat, and has brothers and sisters dressed in crimson, feels a little above such living.

Now, one day this star-fish set out on a summer

journey, - not to the seaside where you and I went last year: of course not, for he was there already. No; he thought he would go to the mountains. He could not go to the Rocky Mountains, nor to the Catskill Mountains, nor the White Mountains; for, with all his accomplishments, he had not yet learned to live in any drier place than a pool among the rocks, or the very wettest sand at low tide: so, if he travelled to the mountains, it must be to the mountains of the sea.

Perhaps you didn't know that there are mountains in the sea. I have seen them, however, and I think you have, too, - at least their tops, if nothing more. What is that little rocky ledge, where the lighthouse stands, but the stony top of a hill rising from the bottom of the sea? And what are the pretty green islands, with their clusters of trees and grassy slopes, but the summits of hills lifted out of the water?

In many parts of the sea, where the water is deep, are hills and even high mountains, whose tops do not reach the surface; and we should not know where they are, were it not that the sailors, in measuring the depth of the sea, sometimes sail right over these mountain-tops, and touch them with their sounding-lines.

The star fish set out one day, about five hundred years ago, to visit some of these mountains of the sea. If he had depended upon his own feet for getting there, it would have taken him till this day, I verily believe; but he no more thought of walking, than you or I should think of walking to China. You shall see how he travelled. A great train was coming, down from the Northern seas; not a railroad train, but a water train, sweeping on like a river in the sea. Its track lay along near the bottom of the ocean; and above you could see no sign of it, any more than you can see the cars while they go through the tunnel under the street. The principal passengers by this train were icebergs, who were in the habit of coming down on it every year, in order to reduce their weight by a little exercise; for they grow so very large and heavy up there in the North every winter, that some sort of treatment is really necessary to them when summer comes. I only call the icebergs the principal passengers, because they take up so much room; for thousands and millions of other travellers come with them, - from the white bears asleep on the bergs, and brought away quite against their will, to the tiniest little creatures rocking in the cradles of the ripples, or clinging to the delicate branches of the sea-mosses. I said you could see no sign of the great water train from above: that was not quite true, for many of the icebergs are tall enough to lift their heads far up into the air, and shine with a cold, glittering splendor in the sunlight; and you can tell, by the course in which they sail, which way the train is going deep down in the sea.

The star-fish took passage on this train. He didn't start at the beginning of the road, but got in at one of the way-stations somewhere off Cape Cod, fell in with some friends going South, and had altogether a pleasant trip of it. No wearisome stopping-places to feed either engine or passengers; for this train moves by a power that needs no feeding on the way, and the passengers are much in the habit of eating their fellow-travellers by way of frequent luncheons.

In the course of a few weeks, our five-fingered traveller is safely dropped in the Caribbean Sea; and, if you do not know where that sea is, I wish you would take your map of North America and find it, and then you can see the course of the journey, and understand the story better. This Caribbean Sea is as full of mountains as New Hampshire and Vermont are; but none of them have caps of snow like that which Mount Washington sometimes wears, and some of them are built up in a very odd way, as you will presently see.

Now the star-fish is floating in the warm, soft water among the mountains, turning up first one eye and then another to see the wonders about him, or looking all around, before and behind and both sides at once, - as you can't do, if you try ever so hard, - while his fifth eye is on the lookout for sharks, besides; and he meets with a soft little body, much smaller than himself, and not half so handsomely dressed, who invites him to visit her relatives, who live by millions in this mountain region. "And come quickly, if you please," she says, "for I begin to feel as if I must fix myself somewhere; and I should like, if possible, to settle down near my brothers and sisters on the Roncador Bank."

CHAPTER II.

CORALTOWN ON RONCADOR BANK.

Where is Roncador Bank, and who are the little settlers there? If you want me to answer this question, you must go back with me, or rather think back with me, over many thousands of years; and, looking into this same Caribbean Sea, we shall find in its south-western part a little hill formed of mud and sand, and reaching not nearly so high as the top of the water. Not far from it float some little, soft, jelly-like bodies, exactly resembling the one who spoke to the star-fish just now. They are emigrants looking for a new home. They seem to take a fancy to this hill, and fix themselves on bits of rock along its base, until, as more and more of them come, they form a circle around it, and the hill stands up in the middle, while far above the whole blue waves are tossing in the sunlight.

How do you like this little circular town seen in the picture? It is the beginning of Coraltown, just as the landing of the Pilgrims at Plymouth was the beginning of Massachusetts. Now we will see how it grows. First of all, notice this curious fact, that each settler, after once choosing a home, never after stirs from that spot; but, from day to day, fastens himself more and more firmly to the rock where he first stuck. The part of his body touching the rock hardens into stone, and as the months and years go by, the sides of his body, too, turn to stone; and yet he is still alive, eating all the time with a little mouth at his top, taking in the sea-water without a strainer, and getting consequently tiny bits of lime in it, which, once taken in, go to build up the little body into a sort of limestone castle; just as if one of the knights in armor, of whom we read in old stories, had, instead of putting on his steel corselet and helmet and breastplate, turned his own flesh and bones into armor. How safe he would be! So these inhabitants of Coraltown were safe from all the fishes and other fierce devourers of little sea creatures (for who wants to swallow a mail-clad warrior, however small?); and their settlement was undisturbed, and grew from year to year, until it formed a pretty high wall.

But, before going any farther, you may like to know that these settlers were all of the polyp family: fathers and mothers, brothers and sisters, uncles and aunts, - all were polyps. And this is the way their families increased: after the first comers were fairly settled, and pretty thoroughly turned to stone, little buds, looking somewhat like the smallest leaf-buds of the spring-time, began to grow out of their edges. These were their children, at least one kind of their children; for they had yet another kind also, coming from eggs, and floating off in the water like the first settlers. These latter we might call the free children or wanderers, while the former could be named the fixed children. But even the wanderers come back after a short time, and settle beside their parents, as you remember the one who met the star-fish was about to do.

It was not very easy for you or me to think back so many thousand years to the very beginning of Coraltown, nor is it less difficult to realize how many,

many years were passing while the little town grew, even as far as I have told you.

The old great-grandfathers and great-grandmothers had died, but they left their stone bodies still standing, as a support and assistance to their descendants who had built above them; and the walls had risen, not like walls of common stone or brick, but all alive and busy building themselves, day after day, and year after year, until now, at the time of the star-fish's visit, the topmost towers could sometimes catch a gleam of sunlight when the tide was low; and when storms rolled the great waves that way, they would dash against the little castles, breaking themselves into snowy spray, and crumbling away at the same time the tiny walls that had been the polyps' work of years. Do you think that was too bad, and quite discouraging to the workers. It does seem so; but you will see how the good God, who is their loving Father just the same as he is ours, had a grand purpose in letting the waves break down their houses, just as he always does in all the disappointments he sends to us. Wait till you finish the story, and tell me if you don't think so.

And now let us see what the star-fish thought of the little town and its inhabitants. "Ah, these are your houses!" he said. "Why don't you come out of them, and travel about to see the world?" - "These are not our houses, but ourselves," answered the polyps; "we can't come out, and we don't want to. We are here to build, and building is all we care to do; as for seeing the world, that is all very well for those who have eyes, but we have none."

Then the star-fish turned away in contempt from such creatures, - "people of neither taste nor ability, no eyes, no feet, no water-strainers; poor little useless things, what good are they in the world, with their stupid, blind building of which they think so much?" And he worked himself off into a branch water-train that was setting that way, and, without so much as bidding the polyps good-by, turned his back upon Coraltown, and presently found a fellow-passenger fine enough to absorb all his attention, - a passenger, I say, but we shall find it rather a group of passengers in their own pretty boat; some curled in spiral coils, some trailing like little swimmers behind, some snugly ensconced inside, but all of such brilliant colors and gay bearing that even the star-fish felt his inferiority; and, wishing to make friends with so fine a neighbor, he whirled a tempting morsel of food towards one of the swimming party, and politely offered it to him. "No, I thank you," replied the swimmer, "I don't eat; my sister does the eating, I only swim." Turning to another of the gay company with the same offer, he was answered, "Thank you, the eaters are at the other side; I only lay eggs." "What strange people!" thought the star-fish; but, with all his learning, he didn't know every thing, and had never heard how people sometimes live in communities, and divide the work as suits their fancy.

While we leave him wondering, let us go back to Coraltown. The crumbling bits, beaten off by the waves, floated about, filling all the chinks of the wall, while the rough edges at the top caught long ribbons of seaweed, and sometimes drifting wood from wrecked vessels, and then the sea washed up sand in great heaps against the walls, building buttresses for them. Do you know what buttresses are? If you don't, I will leave you to find out. And the polyps, who do not know how to live in the light and air, had all died; or those who were wanderers had emigrated to some new place. Poor little things, their useless lives had ended, and what good had they done in the world?

CHAPTER III.

LITTLE SUNSHINE.

And now let us look at Coraltown once more. It is the first day of June of 1865. The sun is low in the West, and lights up the crests of the long lines of breakers that are everywhere curling and dashing among the topmost turrets of the coral walls. But here is something new and strange indeed for this region; along one of the ledges of rock, fitted as it were into a cradle, lies the great steamship "Golden Rule," a vessel full two hundred and fifty feet long, and holding six or seven hundred people. Her masts are gone, and so are the tall chimneys from which the smoke of her engine used to rise like a cloud. The rocks have torn a great hole through her strong planks, and the water is washing in; while the biggest waves that roll that way lift themselves in mountainous curves, and sweep over the deck.

This fine, great vessel sailed out of New York harbor a week ago to carry all these people to Greytown, on their way to California; and here she is now at Coraltown instead of Greytown, and the poor people, nearly a hundred miles away from land, are waiting through the weary hours, while they see the ocean swallowing up their vessel, breaking it, and tearing it to pieces, and they do not know how soon they may

Jane Andrews

find themselves drifting in the sea. But, although they may be a hundred miles from land, they are just as near to God as they ever were; and he is even at this moment taking most loving care of them.

On the more sheltered parts of the deck are men and women, holding on by ropes and bulwarks: they are all looking one way out over the water. What are they watching for? See, it comes now in sight, - only a black speck in the golden path of the sunlight! No, it is a boat sent out two hours ago to search for some island where the people might find refuge when the ship should go to pieces. Do you wonder that the men and women are watching eagerly? Look! it has reached the outer ledge of rock. The men spring out of it, waving their hats, and shouting "Success;" and the men on board answer with a loud hurrah, while the women cannot keep back their tears. What land have they discovered? You could hardly call it land. It is only a larger ledge of coral, built up just out of reach of the waves, its crevices filled in firmly with broken bits of rock and drifts of sand; but it seems to-day, to these shipwrecked people, more beautiful than the loveliest woods and meadows do to you and me.

It would be too long a story if I should tell you how the people were moved from the wreck to this little harbor of refuge, lowered over the vessel's side with ropes, taken first to a raft which had been made of broken parts of the vessel, and the next day in little boats to the rocky island; but you can make a picture in your mind of the boats full of people, and the sailors rowing through the breakers, and the great sea-birds coming to meet their strange visitors, peering curiously at them, as if they wondered what new kind of creatures were these, without wings or beaks. And you must see in the very first boat little May Warner, three years and a half old, with her sunny hair all wet with spray, and her blue eyes wide open to see all the wonders about her. For May doesn't know what danger is: even while on the wreck, she clapped her little hands in delight to see the great curling crests of the waves; and now she is singing her merry songs to the sea-birds, and laughing in their funny faces, and fairly shouting with joy, as, at landing, she rides to the shore perched high on the shoulder of sailor Jack, while he wades knee-deep through the water.

So we have come to a second settlement of Coraltown: first the polyps; then the men, women, and children. Do you see how the good Father teaches all his creatures to help each other? Here the tiny polyps have built an island for people who are so much larger and stronger than themselves, and the seeming destruction of their upper walls was only a better preparation for the reception of these distinguished visitors. The birds, too, are helping them to food, for every little cave and shelf in the rock is full of eggs. And now should you like to see how little May Warner helps them in even a better way?

Did you ever fall asleep on the floor, and, waking, find yourself aching and stiff because it was so hard? Then you know, in part, what hard beds rocks make. And in a hot, sunny day, haven't you often been glad to keep under the trees, or even to stay in the house for shade? Then you can understand a little how hot it must have been on Roncador Island, where there were no trees nor houses. And haven't you sometimes, when you were very hot and tired and hungry, and had, perhaps, also been kept waiting a long hour for somebody who didn't come, - haven't you felt a little cross and fretful and impatient, so that nothing seemed pleasant to you, and you seemed pleasant to nobody? Now, shouldn't you think there was great danger that these people on the island, in the hot sun, tired, hungry, and waiting, waiting, day and night, for some vessel to come and take them to their homes again, and not feeling at all sure that any such vessel would ever come, - shouldn't you think there was danger of their becoming cross and fretful and impatient? And if one begins to say, "Oh, how tired I am, and how hard the rocks are, and how little dinner I have had, and how hot the sun is, and what shall we ever do waiting here so long, and how shall we ever get home again!" don't you see that all would begin to be discouraged? And sometimes on this island it did happen just so: first one would be discouraged, and then another; and as soon as you begin to feel in this way, you know at once every thing grows even worse than it was before, - the sun feels hotter, the rocks harder, the water tastes more disagreeably, and the crab's claws less palatable. But in the midst of all the trouble, May would come tripping over the rocks, - a little sunburnt girl now, with tattered clothes and bare feet, - and she would bring a pretty pink conch-shell or the lovely rose-colored sea-mosses, and tell her funny little story of where she found them. The discontented people would gather around her: she would give a sailor kiss to one, and a French kiss to another, and, best of all, a Yankee kiss, with both arms round his neck, to her own dear father; and then, somehow or other, the discontent and trouble would be gone, for a little while at least, - just as a cloud sometimes seems to melt away in the sunshine; and so May Warner earned the name of "Little Sunshine."

If anybody had picked up driftwood enough to make a fire, and could get an old battered kettle and some water to make a soup of shell fish, "Little Sunshine" must be invited to dinner, for half the enjoyment would be wanting without her.

If a great black cloud came up threatening a shower, the roughest man on the island forgot his own discomfort, in making a tent to keep "Little Sunshine" safe from the rain. And so, in a thousand ways, she cheered the weary days, making everybody happier for having her there.

Do you think there are any children who would have made the people less happy by being there? who would have complained and fretted, and been selfish and disagreeable?

Ten days go by, so slowly that they seem more like weeks or months than like days. The people have suffered from the rain, from heat, from want of food. They are very weak now; some of them can hardly stand. Can you imagine how they feel, when, in the early morning, two great gun-boats come in sight, making straight for their island as fast as the strong steam-engines will take them? Can you think how tenderly and carefully they are taken on board, fed with broth and wine, and nursed back into health and strength? And do not forget the little treasures that go in May's pocket, - the bits of coral, the tinted sea-shells, and ruby-colored mosses; and nested among them all, and chief in her regard, a little five-fingered star, spiny and dry, but still showing a crimson coat, and dots which mark the places of five eyes, and a little scarlet water-strainer, now of no further use to the owner. Do you remember our old friend the star-fish? Well, this is his great-great-great-great-great-grand-child. In a week or two more, the rescued people have all reached California, and gone their separate ways, never to meet again. But all carry in their hearts the memory of "Little Sunshine," who lightened their troubles, and cheered their darkest days.

WHAT THE FROST GIANTS DID
TO NANNIE'S RUN

THE FROST GIANTS

Do you believe in giants? No, do you say? Well, listen to my story, which is a really true one, and then answer my question.

Many hundreds of years ago, certain people who lived in the North, and were therefore called Northmen, had a strange idea of the form and situation of the earth: they thought it was a flat, circular piece of land, surrounded by a great ocean; and that this ocean was again surrounded by a wall of snow-covered mountains, where lived the race of Frost Giants.

I have seen a pretty picture of this world of theirs, with a lovely rainbow bridge arching up over the sea to the earth, and a great coiled serpent, holding his tail in his mouth, lying in mid-ocean like a ring around the land. Perhaps you will some day read about it all, but at present we have only to do with the Frost Giants; for I want to tell you, that, although no one now thinks of believing about the serpent or the flat earth or the rainbow bridge, yet the Frost Giants still live, and their home is really among the mountains.

You may call them by what name you like, and we

50 Jane Andrews

may all know certainly that they are not what the old Northmen believed them to be, but are God's workmen, a part of Nature's family, employed to work in the great garden of the world; but, whenever we look at their work, we cannot fail to admit that to do it needed a giant's strength, and so they deserve their title.

Have you sometimes seen great boulder stones, as big as a small house, that stand alone by themselves in some field, or on some seashore, where no other rocks are near? Well, the Frost Giants carried these boulders about, and dropped them down miles away from their homes, as you might take a pocketful of pebbles, and drop them along the road as you walk. Sometimes they roll great rocks down the mountain-sides, playing a desperate game of ball with each other. Sometimes they are sent to make a bridge over Niagara Falls, or to build a dam across a mountain torrent in an hour's time. Now and then they have to rake off a steep mountain-side as you might a garden-bed; and sometimes to bury a whole village so quickly that the poor inhabitants do not know what strange hand brought such sudden destruction upon them. Their deeds often seem to be cruel, and we cannot under-stand their meaning; but we shall some time know that the loving Father who sent them orders nothing for our hurt, but has always a loving purpose, though it may be hidden.

While I thus introduce to you the Frost Giants, let me also present their tiny brethren and sisters, the Frost Fairies, who always accompany them on their expeditions; and, however terrible is the deed that has to be done, these little people adorn it with the most lovely handiwork, - tiny flowers and crystals and veils of delicate lace-work, fringes and spangles and star-work and carving; so that nothing is so hard and ugly and bare that they cannot beautify it.

Now that you are introduced, you will perhaps like to join a Frost party that started out to work, one day in the early spring of 1861, from their homes among the Olympic Mountains.

NANNIE'S RUN

Can you imagine a beautiful oval-shaped bay, almost encircled by a long arm of sand stretching out from the mainland? In its deep water the largest vessels might ride at anchor, but at the time of my story a lonelier place could scarcely be found. Now and then Indian canoes glided over the water, and at long intervals some vessel from the great island away yonder to the North visited the little settlement upon the shore of the bay. It is indeed a very little settlement, - a few houses clustered together upon the sandy beach close to the blue water; behind the houses rises a cliff crowned with great fir-trees, standing tall and dark in thick ranks, making a dense forest; and beyond this forest, cold, snow-covered mountains lift their peaks against the sky, - a fitting home for the Frost Giants.

Three streams, straying from the far-away mountains, and fed by their melted snows and hidden springs, find their way through the forest, leap and tumble over the cliff, and, passing through the little settlement, reach the sea. The people who live here call these little streams RUNS, and one of them is Nannie's Run.

And, now, who is Nannie? Why, Nannie is Nannie

Dwight, - a little girl not yet five years old, who lives in the small square house standing under the cliff. She sits even now on the door-step, and her red dress looks like one gay flower brightening the sombre shadow of the firs. Her father and mother came here to live when she was but a baby, and before there was a single house built in the place; and it is out of compliment to her that one of the streams has been named Nannie's Run.

While Nannie sits on the doorstep, and looks out at the sea, watching for the vessel that will bring her father home from Victoria, we will go through the forest, and up the mountain-sides, till we find the home of the Frost Giants, and see what they are about to-day.

They have been working all winter, but not quite so busily as now; for since yesterday they have cracked that big rock in two, and dug the great cave under the hill, and now they are gathered in council on the mountain-side that overlooks a dashing little stream. As we followed this stream from the seashore, we happen to know that it is no other than Nannie's Run. And as we have already begun to care for the little girl, and therefore for her namesake, we are anxious to know what the giants think of doing. We have not long to wait before we shall see, and hear too; for a great creaking and cracking begins, and, while we gaze astonished, the mountain-side begins to slide, and presently, with a rush and a roar, dashes into the stream, and chokes it with a huge dam of earth and rocks and trees.

What will the stream do now? For a moment the water leaps into the air, all foam and sparkle, as if it would jump over the barrier, and find its way to the sea at any rate. But this proves entirely unsuccessful; and at last, after whirling and tumbling, trying to creep under; trying to leap over, it settles itself quietly in its prison, as if to think about the matter.

Now, if you will stay and watch it day after day, you will see what good result will come from this waiting; for every hour more and more water is running to its aid, and, as its forces increase, we begin to feel sure, that, although it can neither pass over nor under, it will some day be strong enough to break through the Frost Giants' dam. And the day comes at last, when, summoning all its waters to the attack, it makes a breach in the great earth wall, and in a strong, grand column, as high as this room, marches away towards the sea.

As we have the wings of thought to travel with, let us hurry back to the settlement, and see where Nannie is now, and tell the people, if we only can, what a wall of water is marching down upon them; for you see the little channel that used to hold Nannie's Run is not a quarter large enough for this torrent, that has gathered so long behind the dam.

Peep in at the window, and see how Nannie stands at the kitchen table, cutting out little cakes from a bit of dough that her mother has given her; she is all absorbed in her play, and her mother has gone to look into the oven at the nicely browning loaves.

Oh, don't we wish the house had been built up on the cliff among the fir-trees, safe above the reach of the water! But, alas! here it stands, just in the path that the torrent will take, and we have no power to tell of the danger that is approaching.

Mrs. Dwight turns from the oven, and, passing the window on her way to the table, suddenly sees the great wall of water only a few rods from her house. With one step she reaches the bedroom, seizes the blankets from the bed, wraps Nannie in them, and with the little girl on one arm, grasps Frankie's hand, and, telling Harry to run beside her, opens the door nearest the cliff, and almost flies up its steep side.

Five minutes afterwards, sitting breathless on the roots of an old tree, with her children safe beside her, she sees the whole shore covered with surging water, and the houses swept into the bay, tossing and drifting there like boats in a stormy sea. And this is what the Frost Giants did to Nannie's Run.

THE INDIANS

What will Nannie do now? Here in our New-England towns it would seem hard enough to have one's house swept away before one's eyes; but then you know you could take the next train of cars, and go to your aunt in Boston, or your uncle in New York, to stay until a new house could be prepared for you. But here is Nannie hundreds and thousands of miles away from any such help; for there are not only no railroads to travel upon, but not even common roads nor horses nor wagons; nevertheless, there are neighbors who will bring help.

You remember reading in your history, how, when our great-great-grandfathers came to this country to live, they found it occupied by Indians. The Indians are all gone from our part of the country now; but out in the far North-West, where Nannie lives, they still have their wigwams and canoes, still dress in blankets, and wear feathers on their heads, and in that particular part of the country lives a tribe called the Flatheads. They take this odd name because of a fashion they have of binding a board upon the top of a child's head, while he is yet very young, in order that he may grow up with a flattened head, which is considered a mark of beauty among these savages, just as small feet are so considered among the Chinese, you know.

The Flatheads are Nannie's only neighbors, and perhaps you would consider them rather undesirable friends; but when I tell you how they came at once with blankets and food, and all sorts of friendly offers of shelter and help, you will think that some white people might well take a lesson from them.

They had been in the habit of bringing venison and salmon to the settlement for sale; and when Nannie's mother tells them that she has no longer any money to buy, they say, "Oh, no, it is a potlatch!" which in their language mean a present.

Happily the warm weather is approaching; and a little girl who has lived out of doors so much does not find it unsafe to sleep in the hammock which Hunter has slung for her among the trees, or even on the ground, rolled in an Indian blanket; and when her shoes wear out, she can safely run barefooted in the woods or on the sand.

Before many weeks have passed, some of the tall fir-trees are cut down, and a new house is built, this time safely perched on top of the cliff; and, so far as I know, the Frost Giants have never succeeded in touching it.

Jane Andrews

HOW QUERCUS ALBA WENT TO EXPLORE THE
UNDER-WORLD: WHAT CAME OF IT

Quercus Alba lay on the ground, looking up at the sky.
He lay in a little brown, rustic cradle which would be
pretty for any baby, but was specially becoming to his
shining, bronzed complexion; for although his name,
Alba, is the Latin word for white, he did not belong to
the white race. He was trying to play with his cousins
Coccinea and Rubra; but they were two or three yards
away from him, and not one of the three dared to roll
any distance, for fear of rolling out of his cradle: so it
wasn't a lively play, as you may easily imagine.
Presently Rubra, who was a sturdy little fellow, hardly
afraid of any thing, summoned courage to roll full half
a yard, and, having come within speaking distance,
began to tell how his elder brother had, that very
morning, started on the grand underground tour, which
to the Quercus family is what going to Europe would
be for you and me. Coccinea thought the account very
stupid; said his brothers had all been, and he should go
too sometime, he supposed; and, giving a little shrug of
his shoulders which set his cradle rocking, fell asleep
in the very face of his visitors. Not so Alba: this was
all news to him, - grand news. He was young and
inexperienced, and, moreover, full of roving fancies:
so he lifted his head as far as he dared, nodded deligh-
tedly as Rubra described the departure, and, when his
cousin ceased speaking, asked eagerly, " And what will

he do there?"

"Do?" said Rubra, "do? Why, he will do just what everybody else does who goes on the grand tour. What a foolish fellow you are, to ask such a question!"

Now, this was no answer at all, as you see plainly; and yet little Alba was quite abashed by it, and dared not push the question further for fear of displaying his ignorance, - never thinking that we children are not born with our heads full of information on all subjects, and that the only way to fill them is to push our questions until we are utterly satisfied with the answers; and that no one has reason to feel ashamed of ignorance which is not now his own fault, but will soon become so if he hushes his questions for fear of showing it.

Here Alba made his first mistake. There is only one way to correct a mistake of this kind; and it is so excellent a way, that it even brings you out at the end wiser than the other course could have done. Alba, I am happy to say, resolved at once on this course. "If," said he, "Rubra does not choose to tell me about the grand tour, I will go and see for myself." It was a brave resolve for a little fellow like him. He lost no time in preparing to carry it out; but, on pushing against the gate that led to the underground road, he found that the frost had fastened it securely, and he must wait for a warmer day. In the mean time, afraid to ask any more questions, he yet kept his ears open to gather any scraps of information that might be useful for his journey.

Listening ears can always hear; and Alba very soon began to learn, from the old trees overhead, from the dry rustling leaves around him, and from the little chipping-birds that chatted together in the sunshine. Some said the only advantage of the grand tour was to make one a perfect and accomplished gentleman; others, that all the useful arts were taught abroad, and no one who wished to improve the world in which he lived would stay at home another year. Old grandfather Rubra, standing tall and grand, and stretching his knotty arms, as if to give force to his words, said, "Of all arts, the art of building is the noblest, and that can only be learned by those who take the grand tour; therefore, all my boys have been sent long ago, and already many of my grandsons have followed them."

Then there was a whisper among the leaves: "All very well, old Rubra; but did any of your sons or grandsons ever COME BACK from the grand tour?"

There was no answer; indeed, the leaves hadn't spoken loudly enough for the old gentleman to hear, for he was known to have a fiery temper, and it was scarcely safe to offend him. But the little brown chipping-birds said, one to another, "No, no, no, they never came back! they never came back!"

All this sent a chill through Alba's heart, but he still held to his purpose; and in the night a warm and friendly rain melted the frozen gateway, and he boldly rolled out of his cradle forever, and, slipping through the portal, was lost to sight.

His mother looked for her baby; his brothers and cousins rolled over and about, in search for him. Rubra began to feel sorry for the last scornful words he had said, and would have petted his little cousin with all his heart, if he could only have had him once again; but

Alba was never again seen by his old friends and companions.

THE UNDER-WORLD

"How dark it is here, and how difficult for one to make his way through the thick atmosphere!" so thought little Alba, as he pushed and pushed slowly into the soft mud. Presently a busy hum sounded all about him; and, becoming accustomed to the darkness, he could see little forms moving swiftly and industriously to and fro.

You children who live above, and play about on the hillsides and in the woods, have no idea what is going on all the while under your feet; how the dwarfs and the fairies are working there, weaving moss carpets and grass blades, forming and painting flowers and scarlet mushrooms, tending and nursing all manner of delicate things which have yet to grow strong enough to push up and see the outside life, and learn to bear its cold winds, and rejoice in its sunshine.

While Alba was seeing all this, he was still struggling on, but very slowly; for first he ran against the strong root of an old tree, then knocked his head upon a sharp stone, and finally, bruised and sore, tired, and quite in despair, he sighed a great sigh, and declared he could go no farther. At that, two odd little beings sprang to his side; the one brown as the earth itself, with eyes like diamonds for brightness, and deft little fingers, cunning in all works of skill. Pulling off his wisp of a cap, and making a grotesque little bow, he asked, "Will you take a guide for the under-world tour?" - "That I will," said Alba, "for I no longer find myself able to move a step." - "Ha, ha!" laughed the dwarf, "of course you can't move in that great body, the ways are too narrow; you must come out of yourself before you can get on in this journey. Put out your foot now, and I will show you where to step." - "Out of myself?" cried Alba. "Why, that is to die! My foot, did you say? I haven't any feet; I was born in a cradle, and always lived in it until now, and could never do any thing but rock and roll."

"Ha, ha, ha!" again laughed the dwarf, "hear him talk! This is the way with all of them. No feet, does he say? Why, he has a thousand, if he only knew it; hands too, more than he can count. Ask him, sister, and see what he will say to you."

With that a soft little voice said cheerfully, "Give me your hand, that I may lead you on the upward part of your journey; for, poor little fellow, it is indeed true that you do not know how to live out of your cradle, and we must show you the way!" Encouraged by this kindly speech, Alba turned a little towards the speaker, and was about to say (as his mother had long ago taught him that he should in all difficulties), "I'll try," when a little cracking noise startled the whole company; and, hardly knowing what he did, Alba thrust out, through a slit in his shiny brown skin, a little foot reaching downward to follow the dwarf's lead, and a little hand extending upward, quickly clasped by that of the fairy, who stood smiling and lovely in her fair green garments, with a tender, tiny grass-blade binding back her golden hair. Oh, what a thrill went through Alba as he felt this new possession, - a hand and a foot! A thousand such, had they not said? What it all meant he could only wonder; but the one real possession was at least certain, and in that he began to feel that all things were possible.

And now shall we see where the dwarf led him, and where the fairy, and what was actually done in the underground tour?

The dwarf had need of his bright eyes and his skilful hands; for the soft, tiny foot intrusted to him was a mere baby, that had to find its way through a strange, dark world; and, what was more, it must not only be guided, but also fed and tended carefully: so the bright eyes go before, and the brown fingers dig out a roadway, and the foot that has learned to trust its guide utterly follows on. There is no longer any danger: he runs against no rocks; he loses his way among no tangled roots; and the hard earth seems to open gently before him, leading him to the fields where his own best food lies, and to hidden springs of sweet, fresh water.

Do you wonder when I say the foot must be fed? Aren't your feet fed? To be sure, your feet have no mouths of their own; but doesn't the mouth in your face eat for your whole body, hands and feet, ears and eyes, and all the rest? else how do they grow? The only difference here between you and Alba is, that his foot has mouths of its own, and as it wanders on through the earth, and finds any thing good for food, eats both for itself and for the rest of the body; for I must tell you, that, as the little foot progresses, it does not take the body with it, but only grows longer and longer and longer, until, while one end remains at home fastened to the body, the other end has travelled a distance, such as would be counted miles by the atoms of people who live in the under-world. And, moreover, the foot no longer goes on alone: others have come by tens, even by hundreds, to join it; and Alba begins to understand what the dwarf meant by thousands. Thus the feet travel on, running some to this side, some to that; here digging through a bed of clay, and there burying themselves in a soft sand-hill, taking a mouthful of carbon here, and of nitrogen there. But what are these two strange articles of food? Nothing at all like bread and butter, you think. Different, indeed, they seem; but you will one day learn that bread and butter are made in part of these very same things, and they are just as useful to Alba as your breakfast, dinner, and supper are to you. For just as bread and butter, and other food, build your body, so carbon and nitrogen are going to build his; and you will presently see what a fine, large, strong body they can make. Then, perhaps, you will be better able to understand what they are.

Shall we leave the feet to travel their own way for a while, and see where the fairy has led the little hand?

QUERCUS ALBA'S NEW SIGHT OF THE UPPER-WORLD

It was a soft, helpless, little baby hand. Its folded fingers lay listlessly in the fairy's gentle grasp. "Now we will go up," she said. He had thought he was going down, and he had heard the chipping-birds say he would never come back again. But he had no will to resist the gentle motion, which seemed, after all, to be exactly what he wanted: so he presently found himself lifted out of the dark earth, feeling the sunshine again, and stirred by the breeze that rustled the dry leaves that lay all about him. Here again were all his old companions, - the chipping-birds, his cousins, old grandfather Rubra, and, best of all, his dear mother.

But the odd thing about it all was, that nobody seemed to know him: even his mother, though she stretched her arms towards him, turned her head away, looking here and there for her lost baby, and never seeing how he stood gazing up into her face. Now he began to understand why the chipping-birds said, "They never came back! they never came back!" for they truly came in so new a form that none of their old friends recognized them.

Every thing that has hands wants to work; that is, hands are such excellent tools, that no one who is the happy possessor of a pair is quite happy until he uses them: so Alba began to have a longing desire to build a stem, and lift himself up among his neighbors. But what should he build with? Here the little feet answered promptly, "You want to build, do you? Well, here is carbon, the very best material; there is nothing like it for walls; it makes the most beautiful, firm wood. Wait a minute, and we will send up some that we have been storing for your use."

And the busy hands go to work, and the child grows day by day. His body and limbs are brown now, but his hands of a fine shining green. And, having learned the use of carbon, these busy hands undertake to gather it for themselves out of the air about them, which is a great storehouse full of many materials that our eyes cannot see. And he has also learned that to grow and to build are indeed the same thing: for his body is taking the form of a strong young tree; his branches are spreading for a roof over the heads of a hundred delicate flowers, making a home for many a bushy-tailed squirrel and pleasant-voiced wood-bird. For, you see, whoever builds cannot build for himself alone: all his neighbors have the benefit of his work, and all enjoy it together.

What at the first was so hard to attempt, became grand and beautiful in the doing; and little Alba, instead of serving merely for a squirrel's breakfast, as he might have done had he not bravely ventured on his journey, stands before us a noble tree, which is to live a hundred years or more.

Do you want to know what kind of a tree?

Well, Lillie, who studies Latin, will tell you that Quercus means oak. And now can you tell me what Alba's rustic cradle was, and who were his cousins Rubra and Coccinea?

We all have our treasure-boxes. Misers have strong iron-bound chests full of gold; stately ladies, pearl inlaid caskets for their jewels; and even you and I, dear child, have our own. Your little box with lock and key, that aunt Lucy gave you, where you have kept for a long time your choicest paper doll, the peacock with spun-glass tail, and the robin's egg that we picked up on the path under the great trees that windy day last spring, - that is your treasure-box. I no less have mine; and, if you will look with me, I will show you how the trees and flowers have theirs, and what is packed away in them.

Come out in the orchard this September day, under the low-bowed peach-trees, where great downy-cheeked peaches almost drop into our hands. Sit on the grassy bank with me, and I will show you the peach-tree's treasure-box.

What does the peach-tree regard as most precious? If it

could speak in words, it would tell you its seed is the one thing for which it cares most; for which it has worked ever since spring, storing food, and drinking in sunshine. And it is so dear and valued, because, when the peach-tree itself dies, this seed, its child, may still live on, growing into a beautiful and fruitful tree; therefore, the mother tree cherishes her seed as her greatest treasure, and has made for it a casket more beautiful than Mrs. Williams's sandal-wood jewel-box.

See the great crack where this peach broke from the bough. We will pull it open; this is opening the cover of the outside casket. See how rich was its outside color, but how wonderfully beautiful the deep crimson fibres which cling about the hard shell inside. For this seed cannot be trusted in a single covering; moreover, the inner box is locked securely, and, I am sorry to say, we haven't the key: so, if I would show you the inside, we must break the pretty box, with its strong, ribbed walls, and then at last we shall see what the peach-tree's treasure-box holds.

Here, too, are the apples, lying on the grass at our feet; we will cut one, for it too holds the apple-tree's treasure. First comes the skin, rosy and yellow, a pretty firm wrapping for the outside; but it sometimes breaks, when a strong wind tosses the apples to the ground, and sometimes the insects eat holes in it: so, if this were the only covering, the treasure would hardly be very safe. Therefore, next we come to the firm, juicy flesh of the apple, - seldom to be broken through by a fall, not often eaten through by insects; but lest even this should fail, we come at last, far in the middle, to horny sheaths, or cells, built up together like a little fortress, surrounding and protecting the brown, shining seeds, which we reach in the very centre of all.

One thing more let us look at before we leave the apple. Cut it horizontally through the middle with a sharp knife, and try how thin and smooth a slice you can make; hold it up to the light, and we shall see something very beautiful. There in the centre of the round slice is the delicate figure of a perfect apple-blossom, with all its petals spread; for it was that lovely pink-and-white blossom from which the apple was formed, - a tiny green ball at first, which you may see in the spring, if you look where the blossoms have just fallen. As this little green apple grew, it kept in its very heart always the image of the fair blossom; and now that the fruit has reached this ripe perfection, we may still see the same form.

The pears, too, the apricots and plums, you may see for yourselves; you do not need me to tell their stories.

But come down to the garden, for there I have some of the oddest and prettiest boxes to show. The pease and beans have long canoes, satin-lined and waterproof. On what voyage they are bound, I cannot say.

The tall milk-weed that grew so fast all summer, and threatened to over-run the garden, now pays well for its lodging by the exquisite treasure which its rough-covered, pale-green bag holds. Press your thumb on its closed edges; for this casket opens with a spring, and, if it is ripe and ready, it will unclose with a touch, and show you a little fish, with silver scales laid over a covering of long, silken threads, finer and more delicate than any of the sewing-silk in your mother's work-box. This silk is really a wing-like float for each scale; and the scales are seeds, which will not stay upon the little fish, but long to float away with their silken trails, and, alighting here and there, cling and seek for a good place to plant themselves.

See, too, how the poppy has provided herself with a deep, round box of a delicate brown color; the carved lid might have been made by the Chinese, it looks so much like their fine work. Full to the brim, this box is. The poppy is rich in the autumn; brown seeds by the hundred, packed away for another year's use.

Here are the balsams, - touch-me-nots, we used to call them when I was a child; for, Poor things, so slightly have they locked up their treasure, that even the baby's little finger will open the rough-feeling oblong casket with a snap and a spring, and send the jewels flying all over the garden-bed, where you will scarcely be able to find them again.

Roses have beautiful round, red globes to hold their precious seeds; and so firm and strong are they, that the winter winds and snows even do not break or open them. I have found them dashed with sea-spray, or on dusty roadsides; everywhere strong and safe, making the dullest day bright with their cheery color.

If we go to the wet meadows and stream-sides, we shall find how the scarlet cardinal has packed away its minute seeds in a pretty little box with two or three partings inside; and the cowslip has a cluster of oval bags as full as they can hold.

Among the rocks, hairballs have their tiny five-parted chests; and the columbine, its standing group of narrow brown sacks, which show, if we open them, hundreds of tiny seeds.

But in the woods, the oak has stored her treasures in

the acorn; the chestnut, in its bur which holds the nut so safely. The walnut and beech trees have also their hard, safe caskets, and the boys who go nutting know very well what is inside.

Autumn is the time to open these treasures. It takes all the spring and summer to prepare them, and some even need all of September too, before they are ready to open the little covers. But go into the garden and orchard, into the meadows and woods, and you have not far to look before finding enough to prove that the plants, no less than the children, have treasures to keep, and often most charming boxes to keep them in.

A PEEP INTO ONE OF GOD'S STOREHOUSES

Once there was a father who thought he would build for his children a beautiful home, putting into it every thing they could need or desire throughout their lives. So he built the beautiful house; and any one just to look at the outside of it would exclaim, How lovely! For its roof was a wide, blue dome like the sky, and the lofty rooms had arching ceilings covered with tracery of leaves and waving boughs. The floors were carpeted with velvet, and the whole was lighted with lamps that shone like stars from above. The sweetest perfumes floated through the air, while thousands of birds answered the music of fountains with their songs. And yet, when you have seen all this, you have not seen the best part of it: for the house has been so wonderfully contrived, that it is full of mysterious closets, storehouses, and secret drawers, all locked by magic keys, or fastened by concealed springs; and each one is filled with something precious or useful or beautiful to look at, - piles upon piles, and heaps upon heaps of wonderful stores. Every thing that the children could want, or dream of wanting, is laid up here; but yet they are not to be told any thing about it. They are to be put into this delightful home, and left to find it all out for themselves.

At first, you know, they will only play. They will roll on the soft carpets, and listen to the fountain and the

Jane Andrews

birds, and wander from room to room to see new beauties everywhere; but some day a boy, full of curiosity, prying here and there into nooks and corners, will touch one of the hidden springs; a door will fly open, and one storehouse of treasures will be revealed. How he will shout, and call upon his brothers and sisters to admire with him; how they will pull out the treasures, and try to learn how to use the new and strange materials. What did my father mean this for? Why did he give that so odd a shape, or so strange a covering? And so through many questions, and many experiments, they learn at last how to use the contents of this one storehouse. But do you imagine that sensible children, after one such discovery, would rest satisfied? Of course they would explore and explore; try every panel, and press every spring, until, one by one, all the closets should be opened, and all the treasures brought out. And then how could they show their gratitude to the dear father who had taken such pains to prepare this wonderful house for them? The least they could do would be to try to use every thing for the purposes intended, and not to destroy or injure any of the precious gifts prepared so lovingly for their use.

Now, God, our loving Father, has made for us, for you and for me and for little Mage and Jenny, and for all the grown people and children too, just such a house. It is this earth on which we live. You can see the blue roof, and the arched ceilings of the rooms, with their canopy of leaves and drooping boughs, and the velvet-covered floors, and the lights and birds and fountains; but do you know any of the secret closets? Have you found the key or spring of a single one, or been called by your mother or father or brother or sister to take a peep into one of them?

If you have not, perhaps you would like to go with me to examine one that was opened a good many years ago, but contains such valuable things that the uses of all of them have not yet been found out, and their beauty is just beginning to be known.

The doorway of this storehouse lies in the side of a hill. It is twice as wide as the great barn-door where the hay-carts are driven in; and two railroad-tracks run out at it, side by side, with a little foot-path between them. The entrance is light, because it opens so wide; but we can see that the floor slopes downward, and the way looks dark and narrow before us. We shall need a guide; and here comes one, - a rough-looking man, with smutty clothes, and an odd little lamp covered with wire gauze, fastened to the front of his cap. He is one of the workmen employed to bring the treasures out of this dark storehouse; and he will show us, by the light of his lamp, some of the wonders of the place. Walk down the sloping foot-path now, and be careful to keep out of the way of the little cars that are coming and going on each side of you, loaded on one side, and empty on the other, and seeming to run up and down by themselves. But you will find that they are really pulled and pushed by an engine that stands outside the doorway and reaches them by long chains. At last we reach the foot of the slope; and, as our eyes become accustomed to the faint light, we can see passages leading to the right and the left, and square chambers cut out in the solid hill. So this great green hill, upon which you might run or play, is inside like what I think some of those large anthills must be, - traversed by galleries, and full of rooms and long passages. All about we see men like our guide, working by the light of their little lamps. We hear the echoing sound of the tools; and we see great blocks and heaps that they have

Jane Andrews

broken away, and loaded into little cars that stand ready, here and there, to be drawn by mules to the foot of the slope.

Now, are you curious to know what this treasure is? Have you seen already that it is only coal, and do you wonder that I think it is so precious? Look a little closer, while our guide lets the light of his lamp fall upon the black wall at your side. Do you see the delicate tracery of ferns, more beautiful than the fairest drawing. See, beneath your feet is the marking of great tree-trunks lying aslant across the floor, and the forms of gigantic palm-leaves strewed among them. Here is something different, rounded like a nut-shell; you can split off one side, and behold there is the nut lying snugly as does any chestnut in its bur!

Did you notice the great pillars of coal that are left to uphold the roof? Let us look at them; for perhaps we can examine them more closely than we can the roof, and the sides of these halls. Here are mosses and little leaves, and sometimes an odd-looking little body that is not unlike some of the sea-creatures we found at the beach last summer; and every thing is made of coal, nothing but coal. How did it happen, and what does it mean? Ferns and palms, mosses and trees and animals, all perfect, all beautiful, and yet all hidden away under this hill, and turned into shining black coal.

Now, I can very well remember when I first saw a coal fire, and how odd it looked to see what seemed to be burning stones. For, when I was a little girl, we always had logs of wood blazing in an open fireplace, and so did many other people, and coal was just coming into use for fuel. What should we have done, if everybody had kept on burning wood to this day? There would have been scarcely a tree left standing; for think of all the locomotives and engines in factories, besides all the fires in houses and churches and schoolhouses. But God knew that we should have need of other fuel besides wood, and so he made great forests to grow on the earth before he had made any men to live upon it. These forests were of trees, different in some ways from those we have now, great ferns as tall as this house, and mosses as high as little trees, and palm-leaves of enormous size. And, when they were all prepared, he planned how they should best be stored up for the use of his children, who would not be here to use them for many thousand years to come. So he let them grow and ripen and fall to the ground, and then the great rocks were piled above them to crowd them compactly together, and they were heated and heavily pressed, until, as the ages went by, they changed slowly into these hard, black, shining stones, and became better fuel than any wood, because the substance of wood was concentrated in them. Then the hills were piled up on top of it all; but here and there some edge of a coal-bed was tilted up, and appeared above the ground. This served for a hint to curious men, to make them ask "What is this?" and "What is it good for?" and so at last, following their questions, to find their way to the secret stores, and make an open doorway, and let the world in. So much for the fuel; but God meant something else besides fuel when he packed this closet for his children. At first they only understood this simplest and plainest value of the coal. But there were some things that troubled the miners very much: one was gas that would take fire from their lamps, and burn, making it dangerous for men to go into the passages where they were likely to meet it. But by and by the wise men thought about it, and said to themselves, We must find out what useful purpose God made the gas for: we know that he does not make any thing for harm only. The thought came to them that it might be prepared from coal, and conducted through pipes to our houses to take the place of lamps or candles, which until that time had been the only light. But, after making the gas, there was a thick, pitchy substance left from the coal, called coal-tar. It was only a trouble to the gas-makers, who had no use for it, and even threw it away, until some one, more thoughtful than the others, found out that water would not pass through it. And so it began to be used to cover roofs of buildings, and, mixed with some other substances, made a pavement for streets; and being spread over iron-work it protected it from rust. Don't you see how many uses we have found for this refuse coal-tar? And the finest of all is yet to come; for the chemists got hold of it, and distilled and refined it, until they prepared from the black, dirty pitch lovely emerald-colored crystals which had the property of dying silk and cotton and wool in beautiful colors, - violet, magenta, purple, or green. What do you think of that from the coal-tar. When you have a new ribbon for your hat; or a pretty red dress, or your grandmamma buys a new violet ribbon for her cap, just ask if they are dyed with aniline colors; and if the answer is "Yes," you may know that they came from the coal-tar. Besides the dyes, we shall also have left naphtha, useful in making varnish, and various oils that are used in more ways than I can stop to tell you, or you would care now to hear. If your cousin Annie has a jet belt-clasp or bracelet, and if you find in aunt Edith's box of old treasures an odd-shaped brooch of jet, you may remember the coal again; for jet is only one kind of lignite, which is a name for a certain preparation of coal.

But here is another surprise of a different kind. You have seen boxes of hard, smooth, white candles with the name paraffin marked on the cover. Should you think the black coal could ever undergo such a change as to come out in the form of these white candles? Go to the factory where they are made, and you can see the whole process; and then you will understand one more of God's meanings for coal.

And all this time I have not said a word about how, while the great forests lay under pressure for millions of years, the oils that were in the growing plants (just as oils are in many growing plants now) were pressed out, and flowed into underground reservoirs, lying hidden there, until one day not many years ago a man accidentally bored into one. Up came the oil, spouting and running over, gushing out and streaming down to a little river that ran near by. As it floated on the surface of the water (for oil and water will not mix, you know), the boys, for mischief, set fire to it, and a stream of fire rolled along down the river; proving to everybody who saw it, that a new light, as good as gas, had come from the coal. Now those of us who have kerosene lamps may thank the oil-wells that were prepared for us so many years ago.

When your hands or lips are cracked and rough from the cold, does your mother ever put on glycerin to heal them? If she does, you are indebted again to the coal oil, for of that it is partly made.

And now let me tell you that almost all the uses for coal have been found out since I was a child; and, by the time you are men and women, you may be sure that as many more will be discovered, if not from that storehouse, certainly from some of the many others that our good Father has prepared for us, and hidden among the mountains or in the deserts, or perhaps under your very feet to-day; for thousands of people walked over those hills of coal, before one saw the treasures that lay hidden there. I have only told you enough to teach you how to look for yourselves; a peep, you know, is all I promised you. Sometime we may open another door together.

THE HIDDEN LIGHT

There were plenty of gold-green beetles in the forest. Their violet-colored cousins also held royal state there; and scarlet or yellow with black trimmings was the uniform of many a gay troop that careered in splendor through the vine-hung aisles of the hot, damp woods. But clinging to the gray bark of some tree, or lying concealed among the damp leaves in a swamp, was the gayest and fairest of them all, if the truth be told.

A little blackish-brown bug, dingy and hairy, not pleasant to look upon, you will say; surely not related to such winged splendors as play in the sunlight. Yet he is true first cousin to the green and gold, or to the royal violet; has as fair a title to a place in your regard, and will prove it, if you will only wait his time. He is like those plain people whom we pass every day without notice, until some great trial or difficulty calls out a hidden power within them, and they flash into greatness in some noble action, and prove their kinship to God.

We need not wait long; for as soon as the sun has set, our dull, blackish bug unfolds his wings and reveals his latent glory. He becomes a star, a spark from the sun's very self. If you can prevail upon him to condescend to attend you, you may read or write by his light alone.

Jane Andrews

But come with me to this Indian's hut, where instead of lamp, candle, or torch, three or four of these luminous insects make all the dwelling bright. See the Indian hunter preparing for a journey, or a raid upon the forest beasts, by fastening to his hands and feet the little lantern-flies that shall make the pathway light before him.

When the Indian wants his brilliant little servants, he goes out on some little hillock, waving a lighted torch and calling them by name, "cucuie, cucuie;" and quickly they crowd around him in troops.

And here I must tell you a little Japanese story. The young lady fire-fly is courted by her many suitors, who themselves carry no light. She is shy and reserved. She will not accept the attentions; but when so importuned that she sees no other escape, she cries, "Let him who really loves me, go bring me a light like my own, as a proof of his affection." Then the daring lovers rush blindly at the nearest fire or candle, and perish in the flame.

But to return to the Indian. Not only do his lantern-flies illuminate his path, but they go on before him, like an advance guard, to clear the road of its infecting mosquitoes, gnats, and other troublesome insects, which they seize and devour on the wing.

No harm would the Indian do to his little torchbearer; for, besides the service he renders, does he not embody a portion of the sun god, the holy fire? And there are times, when, with reverent awe, these simple forest children think they see in the cucuie the souls of their departed friends.

And now if we leave the forest and enter the gay ball-room of some tropical city, we shall find that the cucuie is a cosmopolitan, at home alike in palace and in hut, in forest and city. Not only does he, as a wise little four-year-old friend of mine said, "light the toads to bed," but, restrained by invisible folds of gauze, he flutters in the hair of the fairest ladies, and rivals those earth-stars the diamonds.

But it is hardly fair to show only the bright side, even of a cucuie; and in justice I must tell that the sugar-planters see with dismay their little torches among the canes. For although mosquitoes and gnats will do for food in the forests where sugar is not to be had, who would taste them when a field of cane is all before you, where to choose?

SIXTY-TWO LITTLE TADPOLES

Look at this mass of white jelly floating in a bowl of pond water. It is clear and delicate, formed of little globes the size of pease, held together in one rounded mass. In each globe is a black dot.

I have it all in my room, and I watch it every day. Before a week passes, the black dots have lengthened into little fishy bodies, each lying curled in his globe of jelly, for these globes are eggs, and these dots are soon to be little living animals; we will see of what kind.

Presently they begin to jerk backwards and forwards, and perform such simple gymnastics as the small accommodations of the egg will allow; and at last one morning, to my delight, I find two or three of the little things free from the egg, and swimming like so many tiny fishes in my bowl of water. How fast they come out now; five this morning, but twenty to-night, and thrice as many to-morrow! The next day I conclude that the remaining eggs will not hatch, for they still show only dull, dead-looking dots: so reluctantly I throw them away, wash out my bowl, and fill it anew with pond water. But, before doing this, I had to catch all my little family, and put them safely into a tumbler to remain during their house-cleaning. This was hard work; but I accomplished it with the help of a tea-spoon, and soon restored them to a fresh, clean home.

It would be difficult to tell you all their history; for never did little things grow faster, or change more wonderfully, than they.

One morning I found them all arranged round the sides of the bowl in regular military ranks, as straight and stiff as a company on dress parade. It was then that I counted them, and discovered that there were just sixty-two.

You would think, at first sight, that these sixty-two brothers and sisters were all exactly alike; but, after watching them a while, you see that one begins to distinguish himself as stronger and more advanced than any of the others, - the captain, perhaps, of the military company. Soon he sports a pair of little feathery gills on each side of his head, as a young officer might sport his mustache; but these gills, unlike the mustache, are for use as well as for ornament, and serve him as breathing tubes.

How the little fellows grow! no longer a slim little fish, but quite a portly tadpole with rounded body and long tail, but still with no expression in his blunt-nosed face, and only two black-looking pits where the eyes are to grow.

The others are not slow to follow their captain's example. Day after day some new little fellow shows his gills, and begins to swim by paddling with his tail in a very stylish manner.

And now a sad thing happens to my family of sixty-two, - something which would never have happened had I left the eggs at home in their own pond; for there there are plenty of tiny water-plants, whose little leaves and stems serve for many a delicious meal to young tadpoles. I did not feed them, not knowing what to give them, and half imagining that they could live very well upon water only; and so it happened that one morning, when I was taking them out with a spoon as usual, to give them fresh water, I counted only fifty. Where were the others?

At the bottom of the bowl lay a dozen little tails, and I was forced to believe that the stronger tadpoles had taken their weaker brothers for supper.

I didn't like to have my family broken up in this way, and yet I didn't at that time know what to give them: so the painful proceeding was not checked; and day after day my strongest tadpoles grew even stronger, and the tails of the weaker lay at the bottom of the bowl.

The captain throve finely, had clear, bright eyes, lost his feathery gills, and showed through his thin skin that he had a set of excellent legs folded up inside. At last, one day, he kicked out the two hind ones, and after that was never tired of displaying his new swimming powers. The fore-legs following in due time; and when all this was done, the tail, which he no longer needed to steer with, dropped off, and my largest tadpole became a little frog.

His brothers and sisters, such of them as were left (for, I grieve to say, he had required a great many hearty meals to enable him to reach the frog state), followed his illustrious example as soon as they were able; and then, of course, my little bowl of water was no suitable home for them; so away they went out into the grass, among the shallow pools, and into the swamps. I never knew exactly where; and I am afraid that, should I meet even my progressive little captain again, I should hardly recognize him, so grown and altered he would be. He no longer devours his brothers, but, with a tongue as long as his body, seizes slugs and insects, and swallows them whole.

In the winter he sleeps with his brothers and sisters, with the bottom of some pond or marsh for a bed, where they all pack themselves away, hundreds together, laid so closely that you can't distinguish one from another.

But early in the spring you may hear their loud croaking; and when the March sun has thawed the ice from the ponds, the mother-frogs are all very busy with their eggs, which they leave in the shallow water, - round jelly-like masses, like the one I told you of at the beginning of this story, made up of hundreds and hundreds of eggs. For the frog mother hopes for a large family of children, and she knows, by sad experience, that no sooner are they born than the fishes snap them up by the dozen; and even after they have found their legs, and begin to feel old, and competent to take care of themselves, the snakes and the weasels will not hesitate to take two or three for breakfast, if they come in the way. So you see the mother-frog has good reason for laying so many eggs.

The toads too, who, by the way, are cousins to the frogs, come down in April to lay their eggs also in the water, - long necklaces of a double row of fine transparent eggs, each one showing its black dot, which is to grow into a tadpole, and swim about with its cousins, the frog tadpoles, while they all look so much alike that I fancy their own mothers do not know them apart.

　　　　　Jane Andrews

I once picked up a handful of them, and took them home. One grew up to be a charming little tree-toad, while some of his companions gave good promise, by their big awkward forms, of growing by and by into great bull-frogs.

GOLDEN-ROD AND ASTERS

Do you know that flowers, as well as people, live in families? Come into the garden, and I will show you how. Here is a red rose: the beautiful bright-colored petals are the walls of the house, - built in a circle, you see. Next come the yellow stamens, standing also in a circle: these are the father of the household, - perhaps you would say the fathers, there are so many. They stand round the mother, who lives in the very middle, as if they were put there to protect and take care of her. And she is the straight little pistil, standing in the midst of all. The children are seeds, put away for the present in a green cradle at their mother's feet, where they will sleep and grow as babies should, until by and by they will all have opportunities to come out and build for themselves fine rose-colored houses like that of their parents.

It is in this way that most of the flowers live; some, it is true, quite differently: for the beautiful scarlet maple blossoms, that open so early in the spring, have the fathers on one tree, and the mothers on another; and they can only make flying visits to each other when a high wind chooses to give them a ride.

The golden-rod and asters and some of their cousins have yet another way of living, and it is of this I must tell you to-day.

Jane Andrews

You know the roadside asters, purple and white, that bloom so plenteously all through the early autumn? Each flower is a circle of little rays, spreading on every side: but, if you should pull it to pieces to look for a family like that of the rose, you would be sadly confused about it; for the aster's plan of living is very different from the rose's. Each purple or white ray is a little home in itself; and these are all inhabited by maiden ladies, living each one alone in the one delicately colored room of her house. But in the middle of the aster you will find a dozen or more little families, all packed away together. Each one has its own small, yellow house, each has the father, mother, and one child: they all live here together on the flat circle which is called a disk; and round them are built the houses belonging to the maiden aunts, who watch and protect the whole. This is what we might call living in a community. People do so sometimes. Different families who like to be near each other will take a very large house and inhabit it together; so that in one house there will be many fathers, mothers, and children, and very likely maiden aunts and bachelor uncles besides.

Do you understand now how the asters live in communities? The golden-rod also lives in communities, but yet not exactly after the aster's plan, - in smaller houses generally, and these of course contain fewer families. Four or five of the maiden aunts live in yellow-walled rooms round the outside; and in the middle live fathers, mothers, and children, as they do in the asters. But here is the difference: if the golden-rod has smaller houses, it has more of them together upon one stem. I have never counted them, but you can, now that they are in bloom, and tell me how many.

And have you ever noticed how gracefully these great companies are arranged? For the golden-rods are like elm-trees in their forms: some grow in one single, tall plume, bending over a little at the top; some in a double or triple plume, so that the nodding heads may bend on each side; but the largest are like the great Etruscan elms, many branches rising gracefully from the main stem and curving over on every side, like those tall glass vases which, I dare say, you have all seen.

Do not forget, when you are looking at these golden plumes, that each one, as it tosses in the wind, is rocking its hundreds of little dwellings, with the fathers, mothers, babies, and all.

When you go out for golden-rod and asters, you will find also the great purple thistle, one of those cousins who has adopted the same plan of living. It is so prickly that I advise you not to attempt breaking it off, but only with your finger-tips push softly down into the purple tassel; and if the thistle is ripe, as I think it will be in these autumn days, you will feel a bed of softest down under the spreading purple top. A little gentle pushing will set the down all astir, and I can show you how the children are about to take leave of the home where they were born and brought up. Each seed child has a downy wing with which it can fly, and also cling, as you will see, if we set them loose, and the wind blows them on to your woollen frock. They are hardy children, and not afraid of any thing; they venture out into the world fearlessly, and presume to plant themselves and prepare to build wherever they choose, without regard to the rights of the farmer's ploughed field or your mother's nicely laid out garden.

More of the community flowers are the immortelles, and in spring the dandelions. Examine them, and tell me how they build their houses, and what sort of families they have; how the children go away; when the house is broken up; and what becomes of the fathers, mothers, and aunts.